This book is dedicated to my grandfather, Pap Pap, who always had his own way of making sure some of his knowledge got passed down to his children and grandchildren.

Emily Asare

Fishing with Pap

Illustrated by Barbara Ðokić

"Dad, Jack's eating my worms, AGAIN!"

I thought for sure I had my coffee tin of worms well hidden. My name is Gabby and I am eight years old. My little worm sucker of a brother? He's three. I like worms, just not for eating.

We live out in the country, and when it rains our driveway fills with squishy worms. Today was one of those worm days.

"Gabby, I'm going fishing in a few days with Pap. Wanna come?" Dad asked.

"Yeah!" I said. I'd never been fishing before. But what will we use to catch the fish? Our hands?"

"Don't worry Gabby, Pap will show you the mighty power of a worm just like he showed me."

Two days later, on a cool Friday afternoon, we set out for our fishing adventure at my pap's cabin. As we drove I thought about how Pap could always turn the ordinary into extraordinary; like the time of the watermelon seed war.

Before I knew it we were there and I was in my Pap's arms.
"Gabby I am so glad you came!"

After dinner my Pap told us stories of the adventures he had taken with his kids. "One time your Uncle Teddy went fishing with me, and the fish flopped out of his hands. I had been trying to have him get it right all day, but I was so frustrated I broke my fishing pole in half. Oh man! I can't believe I got so upset over such a little thing."

After we all stopped laughing Pap said, "Don't worry Gabby tomorrow, at the lake, I will show you the power of a worm with your own fishing pole."

My very own pole! I felt like all my birthday wishes had come true.

That night I dreamt I was a champion. "And the first-place award goes to Gabby!"

"Thank you my fellow lovers of fishing, this would have not been possible without my pap, who taught me..."

"Gabby, Gabby, it's time to get up. You must've been having an interesting dream," laughed dad, "you were talking in your sleep again."

After breakfast we were ready to head out for the lake, when Pap said, "Gabby grab the container of worms in the fridge for me!"

"What? Why are the worms in the refrigerator?"

"Well Gabby when a worm is cold their metabolism slows down and they live longer. When we get to the lake you will see they will be active again. Let's go, the fish are better in the morning."

At the lake my dad wading out into the water, positioned himself, placed his pole behind him like a batter determined to get a home run, and the line sailed out landing in the water with a plop.

Pap pulled me out of my trance, "Gabby come on over here and fetch me a juicy worm and I will show you it's might power."

As Pap put the worm on the hook I half listened and half thought about the worm. "Pap, are you hurting the worm?"

"Well, yes and no. The worm is sensitive on the outside of its skin, but they don't feel emotional pain like you or I when a friend moves away or a pet dies. See their little sacrifice is what makes them so powerful! Now where was I?"

"Something about a bat."

"Yes that's right, you are going to put the pole behind you, like you are holding a baseball bat, and when you have checked to make sure the coast is clear you will cast your line into the water. Ready?"

Pap had confidence in me and let me cast all by myself! The first time my hook landed in a tree.

The second time it landed on the shore.

By the third try it landed with a plop in the water. I slumped over and closed my eyes. This was taking forever!

"I got one, Gabby!" My dad leapt from the water, "A yellow perch! Gabby you will catch one don't doubt the power of your worm." I wasn't so sure my dad was right.

Soon Pap quickly jumped up too and with grace and ease he reeled the fish in. Pap gutted, cleaned the fish, and placed it in the bucket. If the fish died slowly the meat might not taste as good.

I still hadn't caught a fish, maybe I was never meant to; I started to pull my line in.

"Gabby, why don't you cast again."
"What's the use, I am no good at this."
"Oh, Gabby don't doubt your ability or your worm's power. Try again I am sure you will get it this time."

At first I thought I was dreaming, but then I heard the whirring of my line running out. "Pap! I got one! Pap!"

"Shhhhh!" Pap laughed. "You'll scare the other fish away."

"Wow, this feels like a big one!" I whispered.

"It's a rainbow trout Gabby. Nice job!" My worm and I had done it!

Our short trip flew by fast, but it was the best trip ever. Sunday snuck up on us so suddenly that I couldn't wait to come again next year. I was excited to tell Jack and Momma about my adventure and after a few hours' car ride we were home.

"Welcome home Daddy and Gabby! Jack has a surprise for you," said Momma.

"Gabby got new worms," Jack said.

"Jack this worm has a mighty power. Not only can it feed birds and sometimes little brothers, but it can also help catch fish. And just because you and I are little doesn't mean we can't do mighty things too. Oh Jack," I chuckled, "don't worry one day you will see the mighty power of a worm when you go fishing with Pap."

EMILY ASARE: I live in Victor, NY with my three children, one boy and two girls, and my husband. I have an educational bachelor's degree and a master's in English as a New Language. My every day job, minus being a mom, is teaching. After my grandfather passed away I felt I wanted to remember some of the memories I had of him. I have always wanted to write a children's book so therefore Fishing with Pap was created. Just like Gabby I used to collect worms and now my daughters will go out after the rain and collect worms, too. They are the best for fishing!

BARBARA ĐOKIĆ: She lives in Belgrade, Serbia and is single. She got her bachelor's and master's degree in the faculty of Applied Arts. While she was studying she began to explore illustration and soon discovered that she loved it. She continued to work on her passion as she studied through school. Now two years later she has her own studio where she paints, draws, illustrates and uses oils. She creates personal pieces and uses her passion to help others words come to life.

CPSIA information can be obtained
at www.ICGtesting.com
Printed in the USA
LVHW051131090820
662602LV00011BA/377